MONSTER CAKE

Laurie Lazzaro Knowlton
Illustrated by Chase Jensen

PELICAN PUBLISHING COMPANY

GRETNA 2018

ISBN: 9781455623778
Ebook ISBN: 9781455623785

Printed in Malaysia
Published by Pelican Publishing Company, Inc.
1000 Burmaster Street, Gretna, Louisiana 70053

*Thank you, God, for the gift of creativity.
Dedicated to the little monsters in my life,
Farra and Gwen*

"Oh my gosh!" said Mariah. "The **monsters** will be here in one hour!"

Mariah grabbed a recipe card, measuring cups, a bowl, and ingredients. "I still have a cake to make!"

"Monsters?" asked Brendan. "Preposterous!"
"Don't believe me?" Mariah preheated the oven.
"What's *really* going on?" asked Brendan.

"Tick-tock, the clock is ticking," said Mariah. "First, I need four ¼ cups of moldy-muck."

"Wait one-nan-o-second!" said Brendan. "Four ¼ cups are equal to one cup."

"Not when it's moldy-muck," said Mariah.

"Yes, always," said Brendan. "Mash your four ¼ cups of moldy-muck into this one cup measuring cup. See? They equal one cup."

"You're slowing me down!" Mariah looked at the empty ¼ cups and the full one cup.

"OK. So you're right." She grabbed a jar. "What's next?" asked Brendan.

"Unbelievers don't get to make cake." Mariah glopped two ½ cups full of goop-gas in the bowl. "I only have one hour."

"Actually, you have 45 minutes." said Brendan. "By the way, you know 60 minutes is the same as one hour. Measuring is a lot like telling time. There is one whole hour, one half hour, one quarter hour. . ."

"**Augh!**" Mariah grabbed slug-juice. "Forty-five minutes! You're making me nuts! I have to measure two ½ cups of slug-juice."

Brendan mumbled, "Two ½ cups are equal to one cup."

"What?" asked Mariah. "I thought you said, four ¼ cups are equal to one cup. How can two ½ cups equal one whole cup also?"

"There's more than one way to make a whole cup." Brendan smirked. "Like by using ounces."
"Ounces?" Mariah shook her head. "The clock is ticking! I'll never finish this cake in time."

Brendan zipped his mouth.
    Mariah poured three ⅓ cups of chopped shroom-tops.
    Brendan held out one cup. And mumbled, "Three ⅓ cups are the same as. . ."

"Don't tell me." Mariah pushed away Brendan's hand. "One cup?"
"Yes!" said Brendan.

"So you're saying, three ⅓ cups are equal to one whole cup.

And that four ¼ cups are equal to one whole cup.

And that two ½ cups are equal to one whole cup."

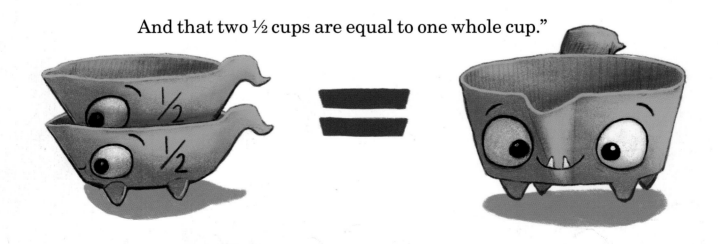

"And now I have only 30 minutes to finish making and baking this cake!"

"**Exactamundo!**

Thirty minutes, or one half hour," said Brendan. "By the way . . . eight ounces is also equal to one cup."

"I'm ignoring you!" Mariah stirred the shroom-tops, the slug-juice, the goop-gas, the moldy-muck with a blug, blump, burp!

"What's next?" asked Brendan.

"Two ¼ cups of dew-web," said Mariah. "And I *know* two ¼ cups will not equal a cup, see?"

"Precisely, my dear," said Brendan, "Two ¼ cups are not equal to one whole cup. They are equal to ½ of a cup."

"No way," said Mariah. "You got me on the one cup deal, but this ½ cup business is totally different."

"Yes, you are correct in your conclusion," said Brendan. "One half cup is just that: ½ of a cup. The only way it becomes a cup is if you had two ½ cups."

"**Grrrr,**" Mariah growled. "This is too much."

"Yes, two ½ cups are too much," said Brendan. "You said you only needed two ¼ cups or, actually, ½ cup of dew-web."

Mariah spread ½ cup of dew-web over the mixture. "OK, this is ready to bake. Set the timer for 15 minutes."

"Your **monsters** are due here in 15 minutes, or one quarter hour," said Brendan.

"Argh!" Mariah growled. "Leave me alone! I still have dishes to wash, a table to set and . . ."

"Your cake smells rather boggish," said Brendan.
"Perfect!" Mariah finished setting the table and
looked out the window.

"Where are your **monsters**?" asked Brendan.
"They'll be here any minute," said Mariah.

BZZZZZZ!

"Cake is done!" Mariah slipped on hot-pad mitts and pulled and pulled and pulled the monster cake out of the oven.

Ding Dong!

"Who's here?" asked Brendan.

"Monsters!"

"Ridiculous." Brendan opened the door.
"Augh! **M-o-n-s-t-e-r-s**!"

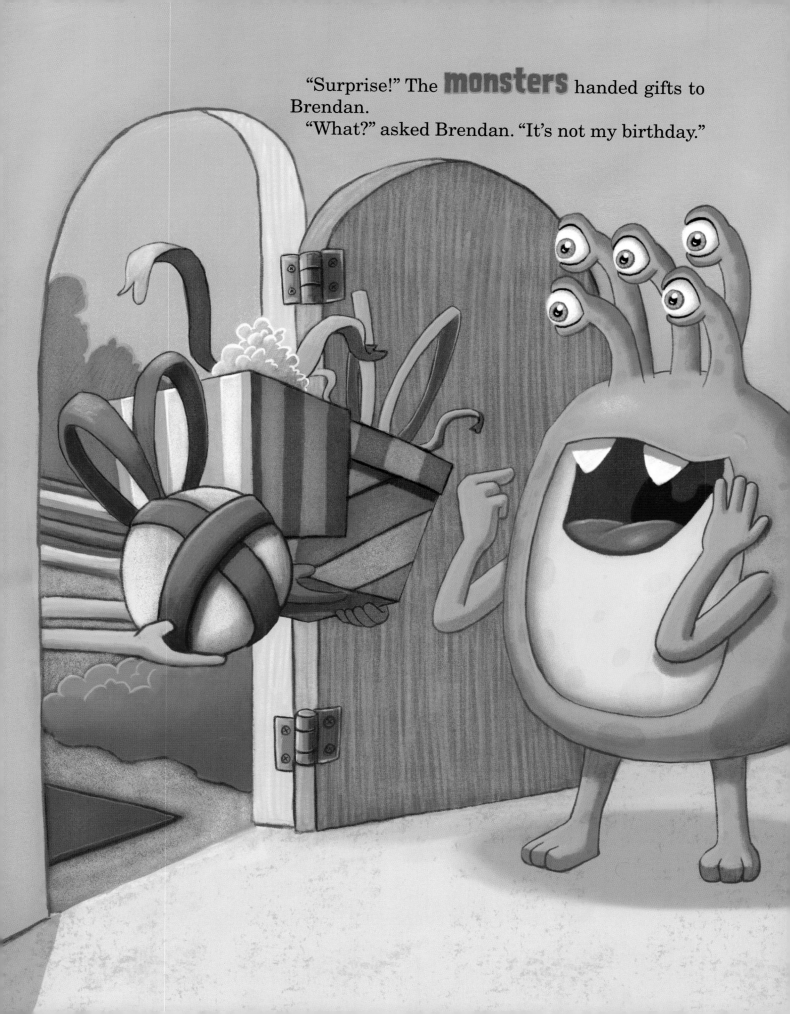

"Surprise!" The **monsters** handed gifts to Brendan.

"What?" asked Brendan. "It's not my birthday."

"**Exactamundo!**" said Mariah. "It's your ½ birthday!"

Monster Cake

To Do Before You Begin

Preheat oven to 350 degrees.

Gather the following items: 2 round cake pans, 1 mixer, 1 large bowl, 1 medium bowl, 2 cooling racks, 1 fork, 1 spatula, 1 sifter, Measuring cups, Measuring spoons, Non-stick spray

Spray 2 round pans. Set aside.

Gather the Ingredients: *Eggs, Sugar, Flour, Baking Powder, Pie Filling or Jam, Whipped Cream*

1 cup eggs (5-6 large eggs)
1 cup granulated sugar
1 cup self-rising flour
½ tsp. baking powder
1 cup pie filling or jam
½ cup whipped cream

Let's Get Measuring and Mixing!

Crack (5-6 lg. eggs) into 1 cup. Put the eggs in a large bowl

Mix eggs on high for 1 minute.

Measure 1 cup sugar. Gradually add 1 cup sugar to the eggs, **mixing** on high 8-10 minutes until frothy.

Sift flour. **Measure** 1 cup flour. Place into medium bowl.

Measure ½ tsp. baking powder. **Mix** baking powder with the flour using a fork.

Mix ¼ cup of the flour mixture in to the egg mixture. Gently fold the rest of the flour into the egg mixture without losing the fluffiness of the eggs. Use your spatula to scoop from the bottom to the top until all flour is consumed by the egg mixture. (*You want the batter to remain as frothy as possible.*)

Let's Get Cooking!

Pour half batter into each greased pan and quickly place into the oven. Bake for 25-28 minutes or until golden brown and a tooth pick comes out clean. DO NOT OPEN oven door until the end.

Remove cakes from oven. Run the spatula along the edge. Place cooling racks on top of the cake pan, and then flip, holding the rack and cake pan, upside down. Cake should release from the cake pan. When cooled, take 1 cup of your favorite pie filling or jam, and spread on top of first cake. Place second cake on top, forming a cake sandwich! Cut the cake into equal pieces and add a spoonful of whipped cream on top of each piece.

AUTHOR'S NOTE

When I was young, my Italian grandmother would make the most wonderful bread. I loved it! Many years later I asked her for the recipe.

She said, "Let's make it together."

I'd been taught how to cook using measuring cups and spoons. When I arrived at Grandma's house I was surprised. Grandma had the ingredients and mixing bowls, but I didn't see any measuring utensils.

Grandma proceeded to make the recipe using two handfuls of this and three pinches of that. The problem for me was that my handfuls were not the same size as Grandma's handfuls! My attempt at making the delicious bread was a disaster.

The next time we made the bread, I came armed with measuring cups and measuring spoons. When Grandma grabbed a handful of an ingredients, I'd ask her to put it into a measuring cup. This time the bread turned out delicious. I was able to make a perfect loaf because I knew the exact measurements.

Let's Experiment!

<u>Measuring Cup Chart</u>

¼ cup

⅓ cup

½ cup

1 cup

Experiment with measuring cups!

*You will need a set of measuring cups and something to measure (rice, sugar, or water).

1. Place your measuring cups in order from smallest to largest.

2. We'll start with the smallest cup, the ¼ cup.

Look at the **FRACTION** ¼. It is a one over a four.

3. The bottom number, 4, tells you that it will take **four** ¼ cups to fill the **1** cup full.

4. Fill your ¼ cup with rice.

5. Because you want to have exactly ¼ cup, you must not under fill or overfill the ¼ cup.

6. If the level is too low, make sure you fill the ¼ cup completely.

7. If the level overflows the ¼ cup, use a butter knife to brush off the extra mound of rice.

8. Pour the rice from the ¼ cup into the 1 cup.

9. Repeat the steps making note of the times you pour rice from the ¼ cup into the 1 cup. Your results: ¼ cup + ¼ cup + ¼ cup + ¼ cup = 1 cup.

Continue to experiment using the ⅓ cup, then the ½ cup in filling the 1 cup.

So: 4 ¼ cups equal 1 cup

   3 ⅓ cups equal 1 cup

   2 ½ cups equal 1 cup

Continue to experiment with your measuring cups, trying out all different kinds of ingredients. The more you measure, the more you'll understand. You too can become an awesome cook by simply following a recipe using the proper forms of measurement!